WHO'S GOT GAME?

The Lion or the Mouse?

TONI & SLADE MORRISON
pictures by PASCAL LEMAITRE

 HAMPTON·BROWN

THE EXCHANGE

What makes someone powerful?

Hampton-Brown
P.O. Box 223220
Carmel, California 93922
800-333-3510
www.hampton-brown.com

Printed in the United States of America
ISBN-13: 978-0-7362-2774-2
ISBN-10: 0-7362-2774-1

06 07 08 09 10 11 12 13 14 10 9 8 7 6 5 4 3

to Nidol
T. M.

to Kali-Ma
S. M.

To my dad.
P. L.

Lion thinks he is the king of the land. He wants the other animals to be afraid of him. When he gets hurt, he yells for help. But only a little mouse responds.

Lion, strutting over the wide savannah,

raised his head and roared:

strutting over the wide savannah walking proudly across the land

Listen Up! Listen to me!

ifs, maybes, ands, or buts questions or opinions; this is the truth

all over of
mighty strong, powerful

whip beat
say do tell them to do
baddest toughest

Shaking his mane, Lion ran through the tall grass.

He leaped over rocks.

He clawed the trees.

He bounded through bushes prickly with thorns.

Suddenly he yelped.
Then he stumbled. Then he bumbled.
Then he mumbled and fell down.

his mane the fur around his head
bounded jumped
prickly with thorns that had a lot of thorns
yelped yelled out in pain

Pain sliced through one of his paws. Pain so sharp he could barely talk. In a little baby voice he whispered:

Listen up. Listen up.
No ifs, maybes, ands, or buts.
I was running over the land.
I ran like the wind and I
looked so grand. Now I can't get
a roar from my mighty jaws
because, because a thorn
is stuck in one of my paws.
Tigers, hyenas, or elephants, too,
please help me out.
I don't care who.

Pain sliced through He felt a lot of pain in

sharp terrible, strong

grand important

sauntered walked

skittered moved quickly

lumbered slowly walked

plea begging for help

whine cry

BEFORE YOU MOVE ON...

1. **Conflict** Lion fell and got a thorn stuck in his paw. Why would no one help him?

2. **Comparisons** Reread page 10 and think about the beginning of the story. What is different about how Lion talks and acts?

LOOK AHEAD Read pages 12–16 to find out if anyone helps Lion.

Lion sighed and tried again and again to pull the thorn from his hind paw. But he could not reach it. Not with his teeth. Not with another paw. The more he tried, the deeper the thorn sank, and the sharper the pain. He had lost all hope when he heard a squeak from the bushes nearby. His voice was almost gone, but he was able to murmur:

Listen up!

Listen up!

No ifs, maybes, ands, or buts. I am the SADDEST in all the land.

hind back

sank went into his paw

the sharper the pain it hurt more and more

had lost all hope thought he would never get the thorn out

give me a hand help me

just the one a good animal to help me
through finished
get a taste for mouse-y stew want to eat me
cure me pull this thorn out

Mouse crept slowly toward Lion. Slowly. Slowly. Then he wrapped his tail around the tip of the thorn and pulled.

Nothing.

Next he gripped the thorn with his tiny paws.

Nothing.

Then he clenched the thorn in his teeth. And OUT it came.

crept moved
gripped grabbed
clenched held

Lion sighed with relief. Tears of gratitude moistened his eyes as he gazed at his sore and tender paw.

Smiling and happy, they parted company. Lion limped back to his den to recover. Mouse scampered back to his nest hole in the bushes.

sighed with relief made a noise to show he was happy

Tears of gratitude moistened his eyes He cried because he was thankful

gazed looked

parted company left each other

BEFORE YOU MOVE ON...

1. **Character** Mouse finally helped Lion. Reread pages 13 and 16. What was Mouse like?

2. **Summarize** Why was Lion the saddest in all the land?

LOOK AHEAD Read pages 17–22 to find out how Mouse changes after he helps Lion.

Mouse feels different after saving Lion. He thinks that he is a lion and a king. He tries to act tough and look like Lion. But the other animals just laugh at him.

The next day Mouse woke feeling very strange. His heart sounded like a drum in his chest.

His teeth felt as sharp as razors.

sounded like a drum in his chest was beating very fast